**Anonymous**

# Intructions fot the Management of Harvey's Sea Torpedo

AF132173

Anatiposi

Anonymous

# Intructions fot the Management of Harvey's Sea Torpedo

Reprint of the original.

1st Edition 2023　|　ISBN: 978-3-38210-068-1

Anatiposi Verlag is an imprint of Outlook Verlagsgesellschaft mbH.

Verlag (Publisher): Outlook Verlag GmbH, Zeilweg 44, 60439 Frankfurt, Deutschland
Vertretungsberechtigt (Authorized to represent): E. Roepke, Zeilweg 44, 60439 Frankfurt, Deutschland
Druck (Print): Books on Demand GmbH, In de Tarpen 42, 22848 Norderstedt, Deutschland

# INSTRUCTIONS

FOR THE

## MANAGEMENT

OF

# HARVEY'S SEA TORPEDO.

LONDON:

E. & F. N. SPON, 48, CHARING CROSS.

PORTSMOUTH: J. GRIFFIN & CO.  DEVONPORT: J. R. H. SPRY.

1871.

LONDON: PRINTED BY WILLIAM CLOWES AND SONS, STAMFORD STREET AND CHARING CROSS.

# INSTRUCTIONS

FOR THE

## MANAGEMENT OF HARVEY'S SEA TORPEDO.

To impart a thorough knowledge of the management of such an arm as the sea torpedo is a matter of easy accomplishment by personal explanation; especially so, when the arm is in the water, and practised with under conditions that would obtain in its application to the disabling of, or to the destruction of vessels against which it may be employed.

But in the absence of such mode of instruction, the following directions are offered, with a hope that they will prove sufficiently explanatory of an arm, which, like other arms, requires skill and aptitude in using it effectively.

By the instructions here given, it must be understood, there are two torpedoes; though both are of the same kind, they differ in construction, by reason of the difference in the position of their respective planes, so that one may diverge to port, and the other to starboard; the direction of the divergence is known by the position of the slings and rudder. There is a like difference in the exploding bolts; the bolts which respectively belong to the port and starboard torpedoes are known by the direction of their safety keys.

The sea torpedo has the advantage of exploding only

B 2

when in hugging contact with the vessel attacked; the
levers by which it is exploded are so placed in relation to

(A)

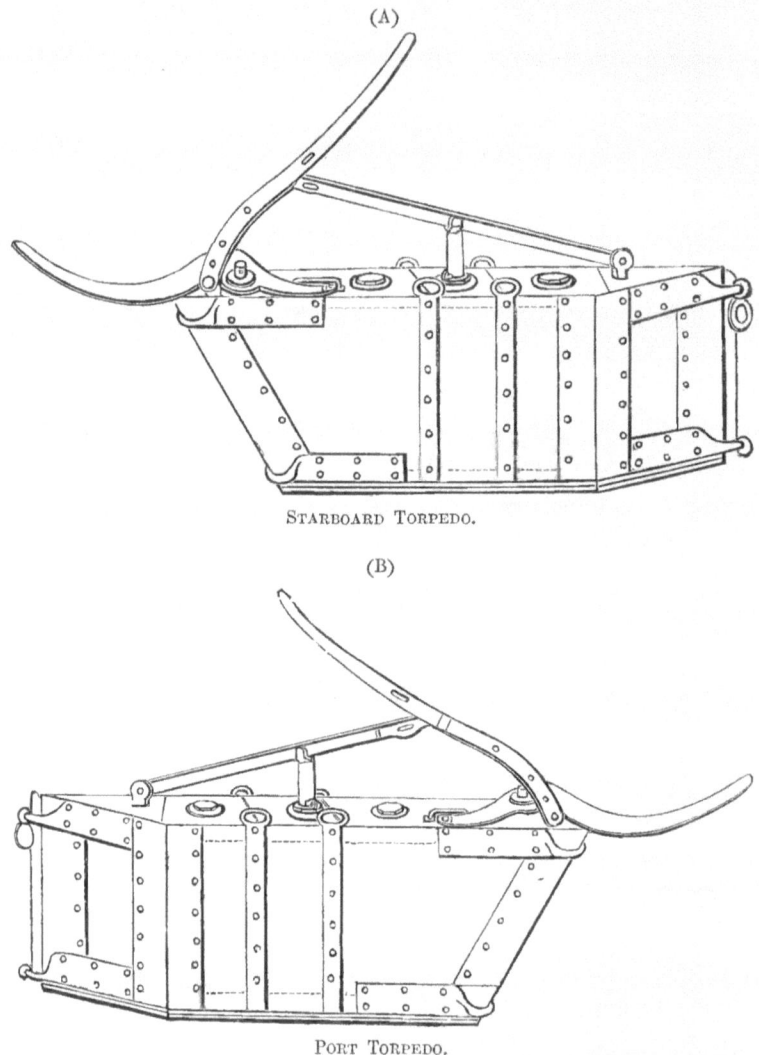

STARBOARD TORPEDO.

(B)

PORT TORPEDO.

the tow-rope, that either the side or top lever is found
invariably to act effectively in forcing down the exploding

bolt at the instant of contact; this has been ascertained by the result of many experimental trials.

The shape is an irregular figure, which can be best understood by reference to the drawings (p. 4). The dimensions of exterior case are as follows:—

| | | | ft. | in. |
|---|---|---|---|---|
| Large Torpedo.. .. | { | Length .. .. | 5 | 0 |
| | | Breadth .. .. | 0 | 6½ |
| | | Depth .. .. | 1 | 8¾ |
| Small Torpedo .. | { | Length .. .. | 3 | 8 |
| | | Breadth .. .. | 0 | 5 |
| | | Depth .. .. | 1 | 6 |

The exterior case is made of well-seasoned elm 1½ in. thick, iron bound, and screwed together with water-tight packing between the joints, also cemented with pitch.

(C)

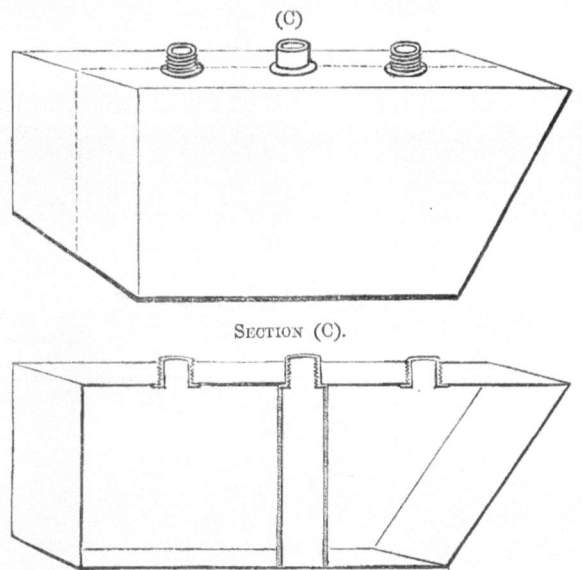

SECTION (C).

The interior case is made of stout sheet copper; the case has two loading holes corresponding in size to two holes in the deck, or top of the exterior case. These holes are made sufficiently large to load with gun-cotton discs, if preferred.

The loading holes are fitted with corks, which are inserted before screwing on the brass cap, to prevent any chance of accident through friction in screwing on the cap ; the bushing has the thread of the screw on the outside for the same reason. If thought necessary, the cork can be cemented over before screwing on the cap, which will render the joint doubly secure from leakage. The centre of the copper case has a stout copper tube, which is soldered to the top and bottom surfaces of the copper case, the charge being all round it; into this centre tube is screwed the priming case. It should be understood that both the exterior and inner cases are thoroughly water-tight, so that in the event of the outer case being damaged, still the charge in the interior case is preserved perfectly dry, the cases being altogether independent of each other.

The capacity of the copper case of the large torpedo is such that it will contain 77 lbs. of water ; the capacity of the small one, 28 lbs. ; from these can be determined the quantity of any explosive agent with which it may be desired to charge either torpedo.

The charges of various powders the torpedoes will contain are as follows :—

|  | Large Torpedo. lbs. | Small Torpedo. lbs. |
|---|---|---|
| Glyoxilin | 47 | 16 |
| Schultze's blasting powder | 60 | 22 |
| Compressed gun-cotton | 60 | 22 |
| Picric powders | 73 | 26 |
| Rifle grained powder | 76 | 27 |
| Horsley's original | 80 | 28 |
| Horsley's blasting powder | 85 | 30 |
| Nobel's dynamite | 100 | 35 |

The above must be considered an approximation, since much will depend upon the labour expended in packing the torpedo.

Some of the powders named have not yet been manufactured on a large scale.

The priming case is made of stout sheet copper, and
contains a large bursting charge, which may be either
rifle grained powder or a stronger explosive, which is recommended.

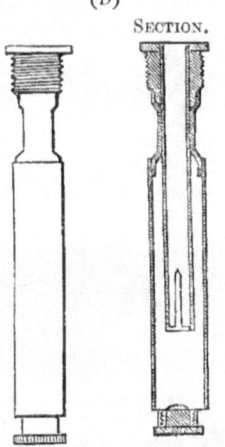

(D)

SECTION.

In the centre of the priming case is a
brass tube in which the exploding bolt
works, and at the bottom of this tube
is a steel-pointed pin, which pierces the
capsule on the muzzle of the exploding
bolt, when the bolt is forced down. At
the side of the brass tube, and near the
base of the pin, is a small hole, covered
with thin brass foil, which will allow of
an escape of water into the priming
case, should any have collected at the
bottom of the tube. The loading hole of the priming case
is at the bottom of the case, and arranged with cork and
cap upon the same principle as the loading holes for main

charge. A powerful spanner is provided for screwing in the priming case
and caps of main loading holes, which
are fitted with leather washers to form
a water-tight joint. The priming case
can be stored separate from the torpedo if preferred, but there is no
necessity for so doing unless it is
charged with a dangerous compound.

(E)

When the torpedoes are being stored, a wooden plug is
inserted into the brass tube of the priming case; there is a
cavity in the plug at the lower end; the cavity is filled with

a greasy composition, into which runs the pin of the priming case when the plug is in its place ; the pin is thus protected from corrosion, and the tube of the case secured from any foreign matter getting accidentally into it.

The exploding bolt is fitted to work with a pressure of about 50 lbs. on the head of the bolt for the large torpedo, and 20 lbs. for the small.

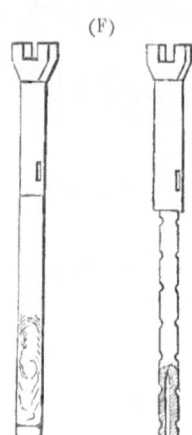

(F)

On account of the great proportional length of the stuffing box, it is quite impossible for water to enter into the tube, and the pressure can be regulated to the greatest nicety by the quantity of thread wound on. The bolts are easily kept in order by turning them round occasionally in their tubes, stored as they would be in the bolt magazine (see p. 20, Fig. Y). The best lubrication for them is hog's lard free from salt, beeswax, neat's-foot oil, in proportion 3, 1, 1.

The bolt has several grooves for the thread stuffing to be wound on, and in the event of its working too easy, a few turns of whity-brown thread on the two lower stuffings will suffice ; should it work too stiff, revolve it in the magazine tube until it works with the desired amount of pressure, which, after a little practice, is well known by the hand. In the event of a few drops of water entering the tube, which has never occurred, a provision is made for its escape (see priming case), that it may not impede the descent of the bolt. The cavity in the bolt for containing the exploding composition is, in length and diameter, sufficient to contain a charge that will of itself

explode the torpedo (see Fig G), without depending upon
the priming case.   The bolts are all the same size, and
differ only in the direction of the slot for safety key, being
port or starboard bolts accordingly.

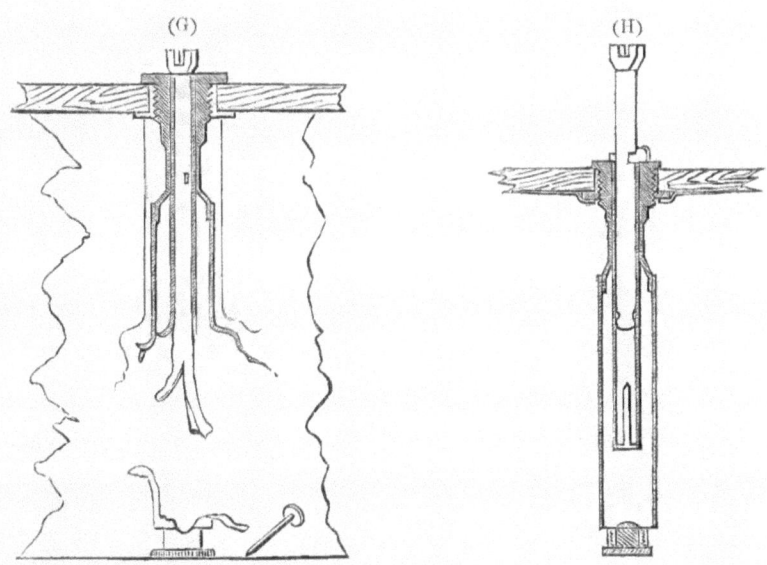

The muzzle of the exploding bolt stands one inch off the
pin when in safety position, that is, when the safety key
rests on the brasswork of the priming case.   This can
always be ascertained before entering the bolt (if thought
necessary) by a wooden gauge forced down until it touches
the point of the pin, which measurement transferred to the
bolt will show the distance of the muzzle when forced
down to the safety position.

The safety key is secured in the slot of the exploding
bolt by eight or nine parts of strong whity-brown thread
secured to the key, as shown in Fig. J (p. 10), passed round
the bolt, and securely knotted in this manner; the parts of
the thread come away with the key when drawn, in order

that none of the parts may be worked down the tube by the exploding bolt.

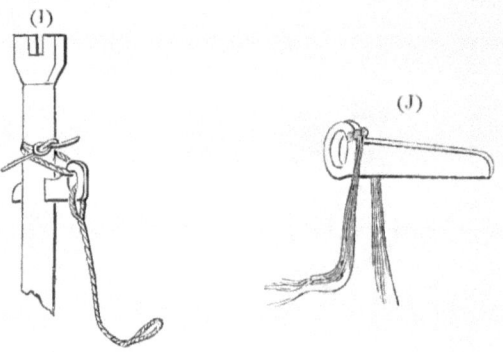

In the event of the large torpedo being cut away in deep water after withdrawal of the safety key, it will explode by pressure on the head of the bolt at about sixty fathoms depth. The small one at about thirty.

The brass guard for the exploding bolt is an extra precaution (suggested by Capt. A. Hood, R.N., Director-General of Naval Ordnance) should any person by mistake attempt to place the bolt into the torpedo without the safety key in its place. It is placed over the head of the bolt and pushed down until the thumb-screw on the side works into a small hole in the shoulder of the bolt. The manner in which this guard is fitted ensures its removal before launching, since the after lever cannot be placed until it is. It also makes a convenient handle for turning the bolt in the magazine.

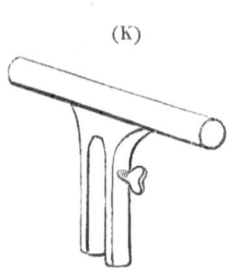

* As the certainty of explosion depends mainly upon the exploding bolt being properly charged, the inventor takes entire charge of this important detail.

The explosive composition in the bolts is powerful and safe; so packed that no amount of concussion can explode it; the bolt must be pierced through the capsule at the muzzle for that purpose. The bolts are hermetically sealed at the muzzle by a metallic capsule, and can be stored for an indefinite length of time without chance of deterioration. The exploding point·of the composition in the bolt is 420° Fahrenheit.

The side and top levers are so arranged, that when driven close into the torpedo, the bolt is down to the shoulder; and, since there are three explosions to take

(L.)

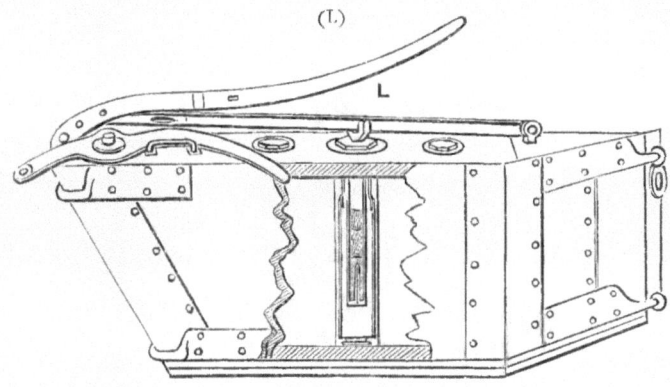

L

place, it is calculated the torpedo will be in hugging contact when the main charge explodes, and exploded by a powerful discharge in the centre, thereby disposing of the explosive force to the greatest advantage.

The torpedo must be closing to the ship when the levers are acting and the bolt descending; no experiment for the force of explosive agents, with a cushion of water intervening, is required. The amount of explosive agent, when in contact, is all that is required, and the torpedo can be manufactured to contain a larger charge, if thought necessary, with a very small increase of dimensions; but the present size is convenient for handling and launching; and if loaded with any of the powerful blasting powders, would, in all probability, prove sufficient to bilge or destroy the largest iron-clad.

The lanyard or side-lever is permanently secured to the short arm of the lever; the end is rove under the fair lead

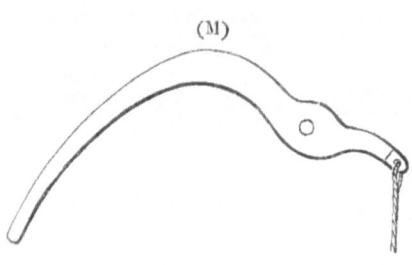

(M)

on the deck of the torpedo up through the brass oval hole in the after top lever, then down under the fair lead (abaft the first turn), and across the deck of the torpedo to the handle, and secured with a round turn and two half-hitches. Care should be taken that the short arm of the lever is brought close into the fair lead, and the lanyard should be

(N)

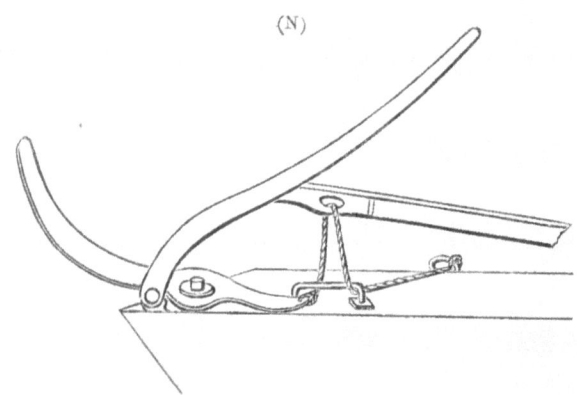

set up sufficiently taut to give a slight spring in the after top lever by the strain brought on it. This lever has a steel fish on the top, in order to prevent it taking a permanent bend.  If the side-lever lanyard is properly set up, the bolt will spring down about one-eighth of an inch when the safety key is withdrawn, owing to the spring in the lever and shrinking of the lanyard ; this brings the muzzle one-eighth of an inch nearer the pin without disturbing the side lever.  The lanyard should be made up like a reef-point ; it should be well greased immediately before launching.

To secure the fore top lever to the after, in order that a back hit may not separate them, the small lanyards, with an eye in one end, and whipped at the other, are first placed over the eyes  in  the  fore  top  lever,  then  rove

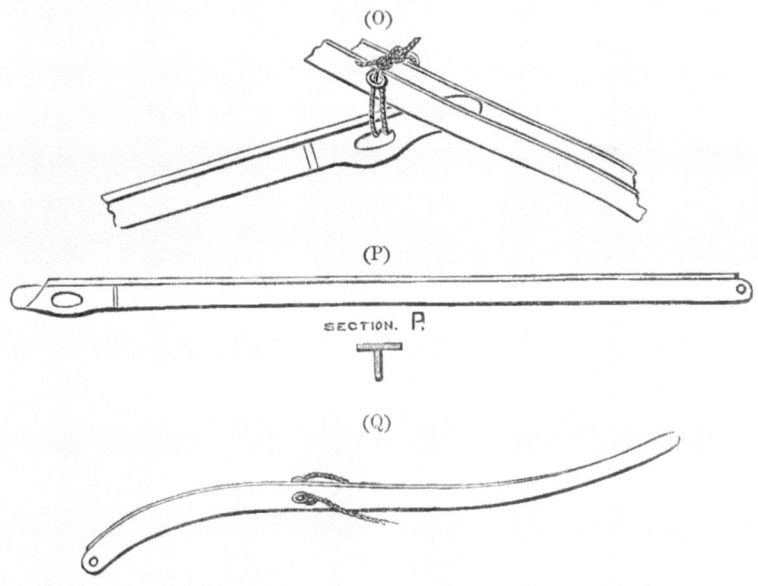

(O)

(P)

SECTION. P.

(Q)

through the brass hole in the after top lever, in opposite directions, passed up through the eyes in the fore top lever, and knotted over it.  The distance from the eyes in the fore top lever to the hole in the after top lever is so arranged that it will not interfere with the descent of them. The fore-locks for the various bolts which fix the levers are made of fishing-line. After knotting them, the ends should be secured together by a seizing of thread.

The handles, formed of iron straps passing under the torpedo, and terminating in four eyes above the deck,

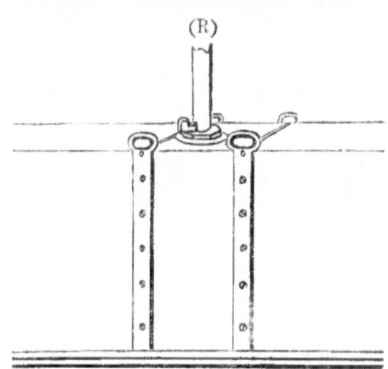

(R)

are principally for handling it; one of the foremost eyes is made use of as a fair lead for the safety-key lanyard, and to stop it to; the other foremost is made use of to secure the side lanyard to Fig. N (p. 12).

The ballast is composed of iron and sheet lead; the former, a fixture to the wooden bottom of the torpedo; the latter, screwed on with long screws into the iron. A thin sheet of lead is always kept on the bottom, affording a soft material for moving them about on, removing the

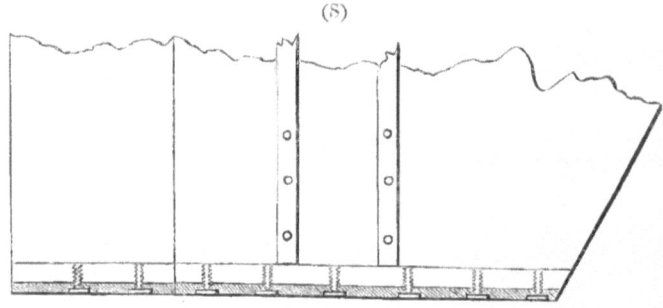

(S)

objection that may be made to the friction caused by an iron bottom in the moving of them in the torpedo-room. By taking out these screws, several more thicknesses of sheet-lead can be screwed on, the same screws binding all together. On leaving the manufacturers, there is sufficient lead placed on the bottom for a speed between three and ten knots. A very large increase of ballast would require another buoy to be strung on over and above the usual complement.

The proper adjustment of the slings is most important, as the divergence depends upon it. The after legs of the slings, when stretched out alongside the torpedo, should extend one foot beyond the stem iron of the torpedo for

(T)

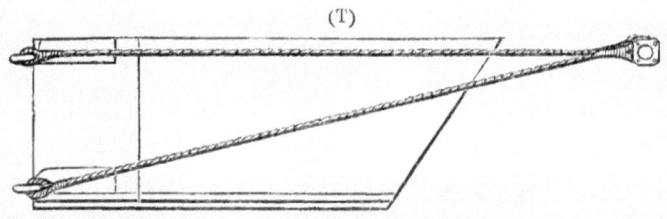

the large torpedo, and eight inches for the small one; the distance on the slings being reckoned from the seizing round the thimble. This first adjustment is near enough if within two inches of the regulation.

The thimble of the slings is made suitable for wire or hemp rope, the fore surface of it being bell-mouthed, to prevent chafe of the tow-rope; the thimble is so constructed that the parts of the slings cannot escape from the groove should the seizing become slack; it will be observed that by this arrangement the edge of the thimble is not brought in contact when rounding the stem or stern of a vessel, the nip after leaving the tow-rope coming direct on to the fore span, and thence to the projecting curve of the side lever.

When all four legs are pulled out, in direction of the

tow-rope, they bear an equal strain; the junction of the four legs should be on a level with the upper towing-irons, at the same time the upper fore span should make an angle between 80° and 85° with the near side of the torpedo. This arrangement gives the best divergence with the least strain on the tow-rope, and is suitable when the

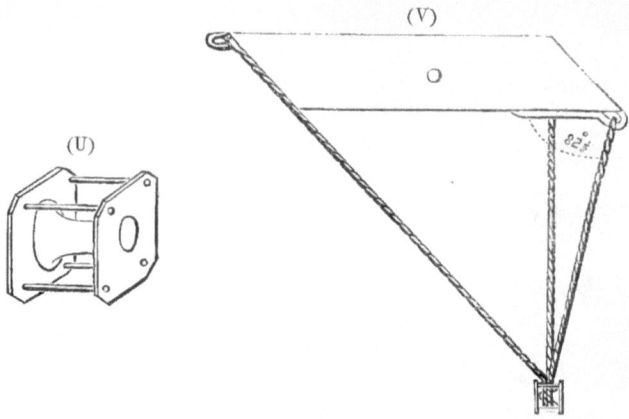

(V)

(U)

torpedo is kept at short scope, as well as when a long length of tow-line is out. The slings are made of the best Italian hemp (not laid up too hard), the rope being of the same strength as the tow-rope; for although in towing four legs divide the strain, yet during collision the strain might be brought on one or two.*

The tow-rope for large torpedo can be of $2\frac{1}{2}$ in. or 3 in. hemp, or $1\frac{1}{2}$ in. flexible galvanized iron wire. For small torpedo, $1\frac{1}{2}$ in. to 2 in. hemp, or $\frac{7}{8}$ in. wire.

The buoys are made of solid cork (such cork only being used as will ensure great floating power after being immersed for a time), it is built up on a galvanized iron

---

* It may be here remarked, the small rudder on the stern of the torpedo is not for the purpose of increasing the divergence, but to control the direction of the torpedo when the tow-rope is suddenly slacked.

tube, running longitudinally through ; on the ends of the
tube are screwed wooden cones, which bind all together

DRAWING (W).          SECTION ON A B.

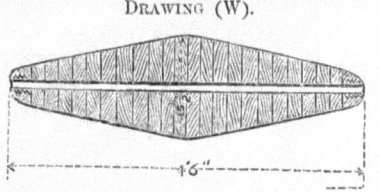 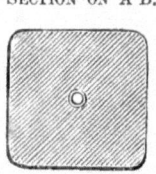

and render the buoy indestructible. The iron tube gives
great facility for stringing on the number of buoys required.

Two buoys are generally used for the large torpedo, and
one for the small. The buoy-rope is of hemp, about five
or six fathoms in length and two inches circumference, an
eye being spliced in the end nearest the torpedo; to this
eye is bent the tow-rope with a single or double sheet
bend, forming the knot by which the torpedo is towed;

DRAWING (X).

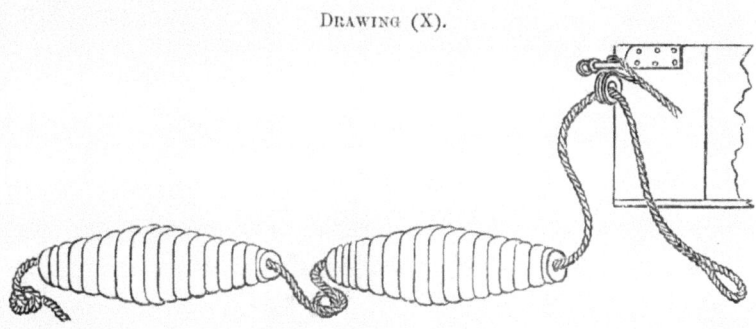

the other end of the buoy-rope is passed through the large
or small ring in the stern (according to whether working
in deep or shallow water), then through the tube of the first
buoy, an overhand knot made in the rear; then through
the next buoy, and a knot in the rear of that.

C

The brakes are used for the purpose of controlling the tow-ropes; they can be fixed by screws into the deck at the most convenient place for command, and, in a properly-constructed vessel, would be worked below the water-line to prevent exposure of the men. They are so arranged as to admit of the tow-rope being quickly veered, and at the same time powerful in bringing the torpedo to the surface when required. Success greatly depends on the skilful handling of these brakes, for in conjunction with the cork buoys they give the operator command of the depth at

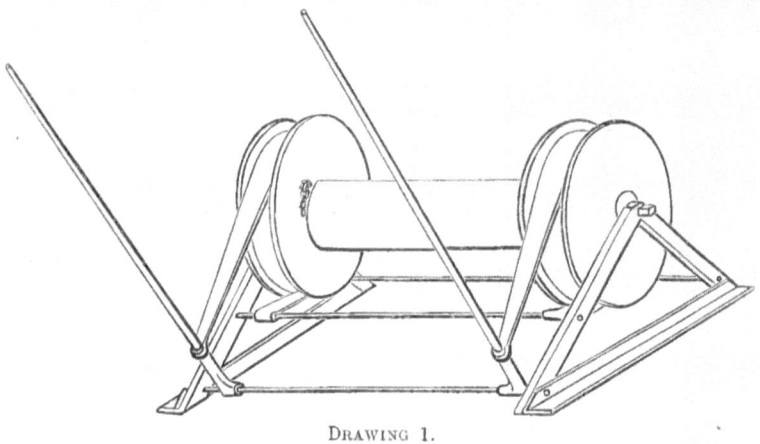

DRAWING 1.

which the enemy is to be struck. The handles on the leather straps are for the purpose of lifting the strap off the drum when veering suddenly, that there may be no friction to interfere. The handles for winding up would rarely be used in real action, and never should be on when veering. Unless a very high rate of speed is required, one handspike will control the tow-rope; the other strap can be thrown off the drum, and the handspike allowed to lie on the deck ready to be thrown into gear, if necessary. The surface of the drum in contact with the strap should be powdered with rosin to increase the friction. The tow-rope should be so reeled up, that in veering the reel may revolve towards the men at the handspike (see Plate 2). The spindle will contain several tow-ropes, that, in the event of one torpedo being cut away, another can be immediately bent.

The brake for small torpedo requires only one drum and handspike. It can be fitted to a steam-launch by placing an extra thwart across near one of the others.

The drawing shows a small brake fitted for the electric torpedo, having a hollow central spindle, through which the

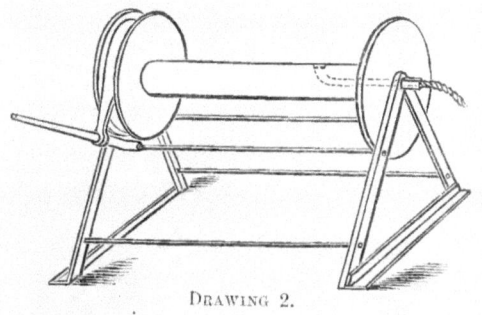

DRAWING 2.

end of the tow-rope carrying the insulated wire is rove, after passing out at the axle; a swivel connection is made with the battery. The brakes, both large and small, are so made as to ensure durability, they being considered a part of the ship's furniture.

Brake for safety-key line is a small reel on the same principle. When going a slow speed, it may not be necessary, as the safety-key line can be attended by hand; but when going ten or eleven knots, it will be found of considerable advantage, both in keeping the light of the safety-key line from dragging astern, thereby lessening the divergence of the torpedo, and also in drawing the safety key when a strong stop is used. The ordinary deep-sea lead line can be used for a safety-key line, or any hemp-rope from three-quarters to an inch circumference. It should

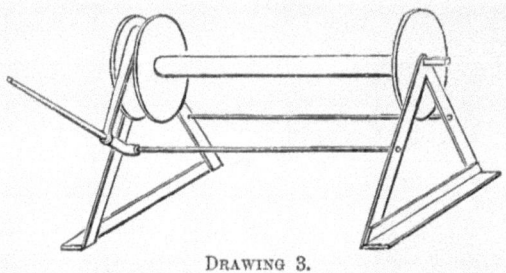

DRAWING 3.

be new and of good quality; for in the event of its carrying away before the stop, it would necessitate the recovery of the torpedo.

The magazine for exploding bolts is fitted with exactly the same size brass tubing as in the priming case; there-

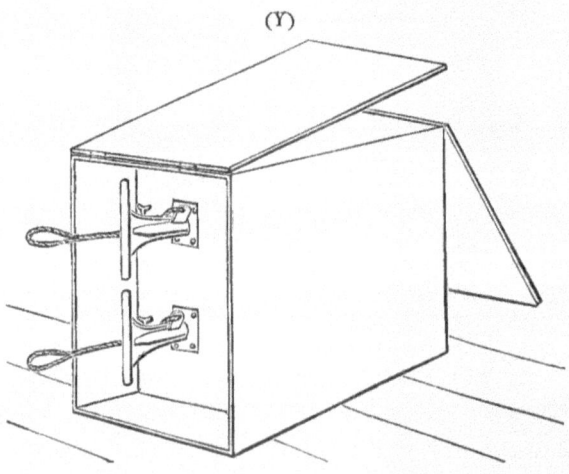

(Y)

fore, if the bolts are kept to work with the proper pressure when in the magazine, they will do so in the torpedo. This magazine should be kept apart from the torpedo-room,

Plate 2.

Keil Bros Lith London.

and care should be taken that the tube is clear before forcing the loaded bolt into it. The torpedoes are then no more dangerous than any other powder case, and, being very strongly made and sealed, are probably less so.

### ARRANGEMENTS REQUIRED FOR LAUNCHING AND TOWING.

A yard across either the main or mizen mast of a torpedo vessel, from ten to fifteen feet above the water-line, is a very convenient method for launching and towing. The leading block on the yard, through which the tow-rope is rove, may be fitted to a traveller on the yard with an inhaul and outhaul, that the distance out from the ship's side may be regulated as convenient.

In a large vessel, the leading block for tow-rope can be fixed to the end of the quarter-boat's davits. The brakes for commanding the tow-rope should be screwed firmly to the deck. In a vessel properly constructed for the service, they would be on the lower deck, the tow-rope having been led along the yard, and down each side of the mast.

A leading block for the tow-rope is placed on the deck by span or bolt a few feet in front of the brake. The safety-key reel, if used, must be fixed in a convenient position on deck, that the man attending it can see how to control it; in a properly-constructed vessel he would be in the pilot-house. The safety-key line leads through a small leading block on the ensign-staff or some convenient point abaft the lead of the tow-rope, that it may be kept well clear of it. The leading block on the yard may be fitted with a lizard, if thought necessary. A sharp instrument should be kept by the brakes ready to sever the tow-rope.

### Preparations for Launching and Towing.

The torpedoes, port and starboard, loaded and ballasted, having been hoisted out of the torpedo-room, are placed on the deck on their own sides, with their heads forward under the leading block, and the number of buoys required for each, placed abaft them, strung together as directed (p. 17) ; the necessary number of exploding bolts having also been taken from the bolt magazine, are now entered into the

(Z)

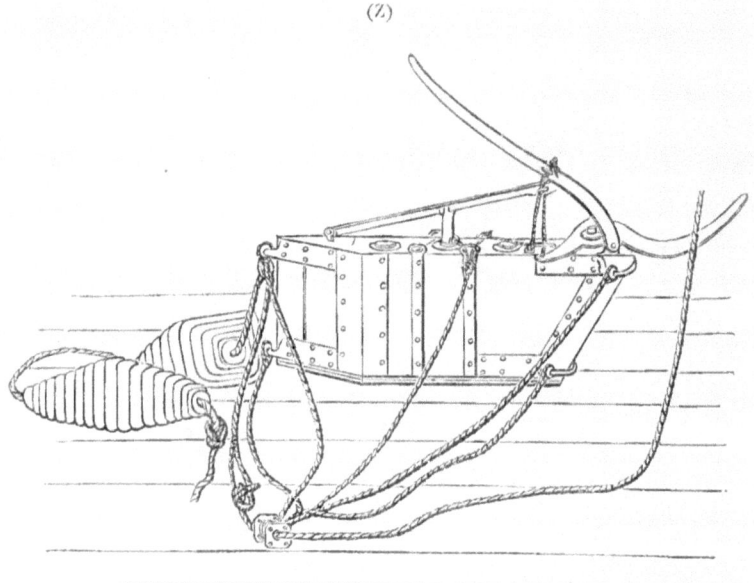

torpedoes, and forced down until their safety keys rest on the brasswork, taking care that each safety key points in the direction of the eye through which its lanyard has to pass ; the brass guard is now taken off, and after top lever placed in the crutch of the exploding bolt ; the fore top lever is now placed on the shoulder of the after one, and the two levers secured by their lanyards, as directed in pages 12 and 13. The eye at the end of the buoy-rope is now rove through the large or small ring in the stern end of the torpedo (see p. 17). The tow-rope having been previously rove through the leading block on the deck and on the yard, is rove through the thimble of the slings from forward aft, and bent, with a single or double sheet bend, to the eye of the buoy-rope. The safety-key line having been previously rove through the leading block on the ensign-staff, and the lanyard on the safety key having been led through the eye of the handle, making a fair lead with the slit in the bolt, are bent together with a double-sheet bend, and stopped to the eye by a split yarn of suitable strength, the yarn having been secured outside the bend. It can also be stopped with another split yarn to the slings near the thimble of the slings. The torpedo is now ready for launching.

### Launching the Torpedo.

The crew having been stationed at their respective posts, the handles having been shipped on the tow-reel, the tow-line is then reeled up until the torpedo will launch clear, and swing out under the leading block on the yard. Hold the torpedo by the handspikes, and take off the handles of the brake. In swinging out, care should be taken that in starting from the deck the fore slings do not foul the fore top lever. The stern of the torpedo can be steadied by keeping a slight strain on the buoy-rope. The safety-key line must be kept clear, and not checked, or it might break the stop and draw the safety key before intended.

The buoys must be placed in a proper position, and hands stationed by them to launch them overboard the instant the torpedo takes the water. It would be better to stop the screw, if circumstances would allow of it, when lowering the torpedo and buoys into the water, to prevent the chance of the buoys fouling the screw. The torpedo, on reaching the water, will *immediately* diverge clear of the ship; the buoys being launched, as the strain comes on the buoy-rope, they will be towed clear away from the screw, and full speed may be put on at once. The men at the handspikes must veer steadily, occasionally checking the torpedo, that it may be kept near the surface, and not allowed to dive, which it will do if the tow-rope is slacked up altogether, and then a sudden strain brought on it.

Eventually it will come to the surface, when the bow is pointed up by the strain on the tow-rope; greater the speed the more quickly will it be brought to the surface. In shallow water this should be particularly attended to, as in diving it might strike the bottom and injure the levers;

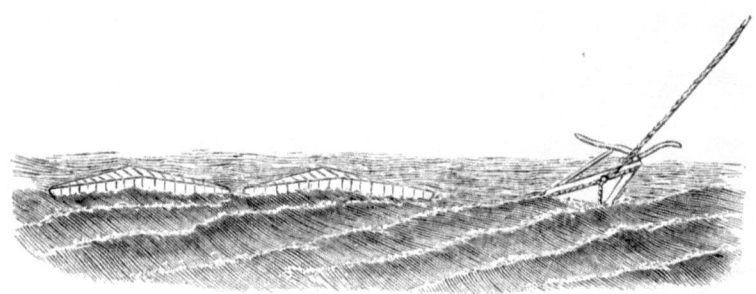

DRAWING 4.

and if the safety key has been withdrawn, explode; moreover it brings an undue strain on the tow-rope. The torpedo can now be gradually veered out to the distance required, the safety-key line so attended, that a sufficient strain is kept on it as not to allow of a long bight of line dragging astern of the torpedo; at the same time having due regard to the strength of the yarn by which the line is stopped to the handle of the torpedo. The distance veered must depend upon the nature of attack. The tow-line should be marked with knots every ten fathoms; under some circumstances the torpedo would be close to the ship until passing the enemy (*see* Tactics); at other times veered to 40 fathoms it will be found most suitable. The full divergence of 45° is obtained up to 50 fathoms, beyond that the bight of the tow-rope in the water drags the torpedo astern unless the tow-rope is triced much higher up, which has its disadvantage; 40 to 50 fathoms of tow-rope gives the best command of the torpedo, veering 2 or 3 fathoms of tow-line suddenly will always sink the torpedo some feet below the surface. Should it become necessary to use the torpedoes with a stern-board they can be so used, but in this case the port torpedo is used on the starboard bow and starboard on the port; all other arrangements being exactly the same. In rough weather, advantage should be taken of the roll, and the torpedo allowed to swing out from the yard, and be let go by the run, checking the tow-rope immediately the torpedo is in the water. It is not absolutely necessary to ease the vessel when launching, the torpedo can be launched at full speed. In the event of its being found necessary to cut adrift the torpedo, in consequence of coming suddenly across a friendly vessel, the tow-rope should be cut near the brake, and if the buoy-rope has been rove through the large stern-ring, the torpedo will sink and be lost, the buoy only remaining. If the buoy-rope has been rove through the small stern-ring, the torpedo will be suspended by the buoy-rope; and should the safety key not have been withdrawn, can be recovered with safety. In the event of wishing to recover it when the buoy-rope has been rove through the large ring, a toggle must be lashed on the tow-rope abaft the leading block on the yard, when it can be recovered by the buoy-rope; as a general rule, it will however be found best to expend the torpedo, and not attempt its recovery. By slacking the tow-rope roundly and stopping the vessel, a friendly ship can pass over the bight of the tow-rope without striking the torpedo; but this is rather a delicate operation, particularly if the safety key has been withdrawn.

### Recovering the Torpedo.

Should the safety key have been withdrawn, great caution must be used.

Tongs, for going round the upper part of the bolt, to take the place of the safety key, when once clasped and secured

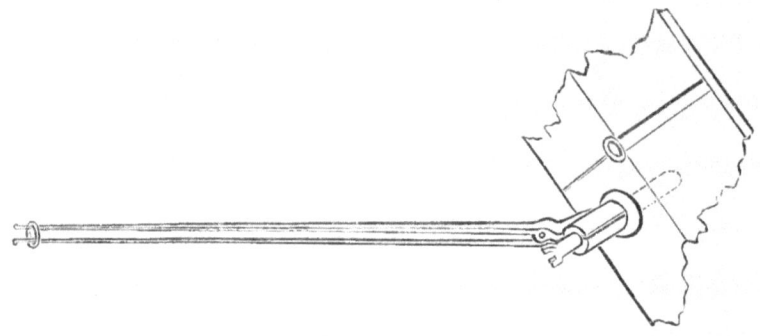

Drawing 5.

round the bolt, render the torpedo safe to handle; this could only be done from a boat. With the safety key in, there is no danger in hooking it inboard again by its own tow-rope, and hoisting up the buoys at the same time with a grapnel.

### Torpedo arranged to Explode by Electricity.

To substitute the electrical method of firing the torpedo for the mechanical one, all that will be necessary is to unscrew the priming case from the centre hole of the mechanical torpedo, and screw in the electrical arrangement which contains McEvoy's patent circuit-closer, especially adapted by him to suit this particular torpedo.

The electrical arrangement has its own exploding bolt, which differs from the other only below the safety key, which key is fitted and worked in the same manner as the mechanical one, in order that the electrical arrangement might not be disturbed by an accidental blow when launching. The insulated conducting wire is carried along the whole length of the tow-rope in the centre, forming a core. The tow-rope, as in the mechanical one, is bent on to the hemp buoy-rope by a sheet bend, the strands at the end are then unlaid, sufficiently so to form a connection between the insulated wire in the tow-rope and that projecting from the centre hole of the torpedo; this connection can be best made with McEvoy's patent jointer. The other end of the tow-rope on the barrel of the brake passes through the hollow spindle of the brake at one extremity and is connected with the constant battery, which must be suitable for heating platinum at the distance of 100 fathoms, the return circuit being by the water. The levers act in the same manner as in the mechanical one, forcing down the bolt and thereby closing the circuit through the fuze and exploding the torpedo.

This system of exploding the torpedo may be preferred in rivers or shallow water, where it would be considered dangerous to leave a mechanical torpedo at the bottom;

but it cannot be reckoned upon with the same certainty as the mechanical one. It is necessarily more costly, complicated, and delicate; the two latter conditions rendering it unsuited for the rough work it will have to encounter.

The torpedo being provided with this centre tube in addition to the usual priming case, admits of its being used upon an emergency, special ones not being at hand, for various other purposes, *viz.* clearing away obstructions; as land torpedoes; as stationary torpedoes, provided they are not to remain a very long time in the water. In these cases the ordinary insulated wire and jointers are all that is required. If required to be fired at will, it will be only necessary to force down the bolt sufficiently to close the circuit through the fuze and then secure it. If to be self-acting, leave the bolt up in its position, as when working at sea, to be acted upon by pressure.

### Description of Capt. C. A. McEvoy's Circuit-closing Arrangement for Harvey's Sea Torpedo.

Fig. 1.—An exterior tube, $aa$; screw-head, $\bar{a}$; interior tube, $b$; intermediate tube, $d$; firing bolt, $e$; spindle, $f$; long brass spiral spring, $g$; short spiral spring, $h$; socket for spindle, $ii$; insulated wire from battery, $kk$; insulated terminal, $l$; electric fuze, $m$; priming space, $nn$; charging hole, $o$; insulated bridge, $p$; metal bridge, $u$.

The electric wire $kk$ passes through the screw-head $\bar{a}$ of external tube $aa$, and winding spirally around the intermediate tube $d$, terminates in a connection with the insulated bridge $p$ at $s$. The intermediate tube $d$ is attached to the head of the spindle $f$ at $t$. When pressure is brought to bear on the firing bolt $e$, the spindle $f$ is forced down, and carries with it the insulated bridge $p$, until the bridge touches the insulated terminal $l$. It will be seen that the

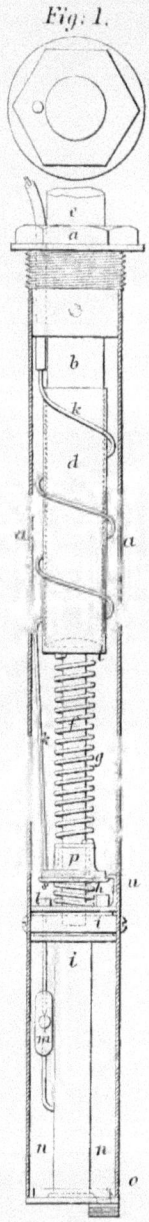

*Fig: 1.*

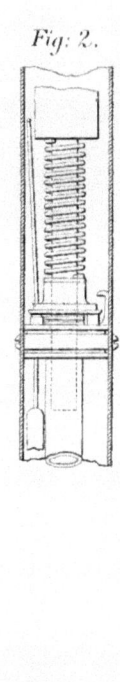

*Fig: 2.*

London: E. & F. N. Spon, 48, Charing Cross.                    Kell, Bros Lith.

long spiral spring $g$ and short spiral spring $h$ serve to support the spindle $f$, and keep the bridge $p$ off the terminal $l$ until they are forced into contact. Whilst the insulated bridge $p$ remains above the insulated terminal, the former is in constant contact with the metal bridge $u$; but this contact is broken when the metal bridge moves downward and before it makes contact with the insulated terminal $l$. When the insulated bridge $p$ is in contact with the metal bridge $u$, the electric fuze is out of circuit; and a current sent through the torpedo will return by way of the earth without firing the torpedo; but when contact with the metal bridge $u$ is broken, and contact with the insulated terminal $l$ is made, the current is directed through the electric fuze, and the torpedo fired.

The priming in the tube is sufficient to rupture the tubes and ignite the charge in the torpedo.

Fig. 2 shows a section of the circuit-closer, with the spiral spring slightly compressed, and the insulated bridge in contact with the insulated terminal, and the circuit closed. By dispensing with the electric fuze, and using in its place a piece of copper wire, any number of experiments may be made with an uncharged torpedo without adjustment or manipulation of any kind; it only being necessary to attach to the return wire near the battery a galvanometer or electric fuze to indicate the time of the impact.

The torpedoes here described are manufactured by J. Vavasseur and Co., at the London Ordnance Works; at which establishment the inventor has every facility in the supervision of the various details in the construction of the torpedoes, buoys, and brakes. Such supervision of the torpedoes and their equipments is highly essential to secure safety and efficiency.

## TACTICS.

TORPEDO vessels should, as a rule, attack under the cover of darkness. By the experience gained in blockade running in the late American conflict, we are assured that a vessel in rapid motion can, when it is dark, pass with impunity close under the fire of hostile vessels, armed with cannon.

In the more early stage of the torpedo, the tactics of vessels armed with torpedoes embraced modes of attack that are not now entertained. So general is becoming the use of torpedoes as a means both of defence and offence, that vessels, which may be at anchor or moored in a harbour or roadstead, would be protected by stationary torpedoes; the use of which admits also of vessels, when at anchor or moored, protecting themselves by placing a web of torpedoes in such manner as to render the attack of a hostile vessel or boats extremely hazardous, and therefore not likely to be attempted. But in the event of a vessel being at anchor in a harbour or roadstead unprotected, she could be attacked, as shown in the illustration of Tactics, under such conditions. As, however, vessels armed with torpedoes are intended to work the arm against vessels at sea or in motion, the management of the torpedo in so attacking vessels is the more important part of the code of Tactics.

It should be here remarked, that with a view to simplicity, the explanations will be confined to a single steamer, the attacking vessel adapted to the service of the arm in question, and confined also to a single vessel, the object of attack.

Plate 4

CASE 1.— ATTACKING A VESSEL MOORED HEAD AND STERN.

## CASE 1.

### ATTACKING A VESSEL MOORED HEAD AND STERN.

In this case the torpedo vessel steers in for the bow or quarter of the vessel attacked, according to the direction of the current, and on the side approached launches the torpedo between the moorings as at A ; leaving the tow-rope slack, the torpedo vessel proceeds ahead or astern against the current, and when at a sufficient distance off, the tow-rope is held fast, which will cause the torpedo to diverge into contact with the vessel attacked, as shown by the drawing.

## CASE 2.

ATTACKING A VESSEL AT ANCHOR BY CROSSING THE BOW.

In this case, the torpedo is sufficiently diverged when near to the vessel with a good scope of tow-rope out. After having crossed her bow, proceeding onwards, the tow-rope will be brought obliquely across her cable, and the torpedo will swing into her, as shown in the drawing. It may be here remarked that, in all cases, the depth of explosion can be obtained by the sudden slacking of the tow-rope ; and the tow-rope, once under the keel, causes the torpedo to be hauled down near to it before exploding.

CASE 2.— ATTACKING A VESSEL AT ANCHOR BY CROSSING THE BOW

Plate 6.

CASE 3.—ATTACKING A VESSEL AT ANCHOR BY PASSING ON EITHER SIDE

Kell Bros. lith. London.

## CASE 3.

ATTACKING A VESSEL AT ANCHOR BY PASSING ON EITHER SIDE
DETERMINED UPON, COMING UP FROM THE STERN.

In this case, the torpedo is launched when on the quarter
of the vessel attacked, as at A, the tow-rope left slack.
After steaming ahead some distance, hold fast the tow-
rope, when, by continuing to steam on, the torpedo will
diverge into contact with the bottom of the vessel attacked,
as shown in the drawing. *When skilfully performed*, the
total destruction of the enemy is certain, since the torpedo
is springing from a depth to the surface, and will, in consequence, strike near the keel. The torpedo vessel can pass
at her greatest speed, and, if thought necessary, near
enough to clear away any of the ordinary obstructions, such
as booms, nets, &c.

## CASE 4.

ATTACKING A VESSEL AT ANCHOR BY COMING UP RIGHT ASTERN AND
THEN PASSING ON EITHER SIDE.

In this case, having determined upon the side it is desirable to pass, a torpedo is launched accordingly. When near the vessel, the torpedo is sufficiently diverged, and the torpedo vessel passing onwards ahead, the torpedo is brought under the run or bottom of the vessel attacked, as shown by the drawing.

CASE 4.—ATTACKING A VESSEL AT ANCHOR COMING UP FROM ASTERN
AND THEN PASSING ON EITHER SIDE

Kell Bros Lith. London.

Plate 8.

CASE 5. PASSING BETWEEN TWO VESSELS AT ANCHOR

Neff Bros. lith. London.

## CASE 5.

PASSING DOWN BETWEEN TWO LINES OF VESSELS AT ANCHOR, AND
DESTROYING THEM ON EITHER SIDE.

In this case, it would be impossible to fire at the torpedo
vessel for fear of injury to their friends. Two or more
torpedo vessels following each other with preconcerted
signals would cause great destruction.

## CASE 6.

### ATTACKING A VESSEL IN MOTION BY COMING DOWN FROM RIGHT AHEAD.

In this case, two torpedoes are launched, port and starboard, each diverging to its full extent; when passing the vessel attacked, one or the other of the tow-ropes is brought across the cut-water, and by the simultaneous motion of the two vessels in opposite directions, the torpedo is brought alongside of or under the bottom of the vessel attacked, as shown by the drawing. The torpedo vessel should keep the masts of her enemy in one until close to, when either torpedo will be used, according to the movement of the enemy. At the time of the tow-rope taking the cut-water, the brake is suddenly eased up; the tow-rope will then pass under the bottom, when, by checking the tow-rope, the torpedo will be hauled under the bottom.

Plate 9.

CASE 6. ATTACKING A VESSEL IN MOTION COMING DOWN FROM AHEAD

Plate 10

Z Incs.lith. London.

CASE 7 ATTACKING A VESSEL IN MOTION COMING UP FROM ASTERN

## CASE 7.

ATTACKING A VESSEL IN MOTION, COMING UP TO HER FROM RIGHT
ASTERN.

In this case, two torpedoes are launched and diverged, as
in Case 6; and in this case it is assumed that the torpedo
vessel can outspeed the vessel attacked, which will enable
her to bring a torpedo under the run of the vessel attacked,
as shown by the drawing.

## CASE 8.

IF CHASED BY A HOSTILE VESSEL, AND IT IS DEEMED UNADVISABLE
TO FACE HER AND PROCEED AS IN CASE 6.

In this case, veer a torpedo astern, having first obtained a position a little on the bow of the chasing vessel. When it is known, by the length of the tow-rope out, that the torpedo is about abreast of her bow, hold fast the tow-rope, which will cause the torpedo to diverge, and be brought into contact, as shown in the drawing. As a last resort, drop spanned torpedoes.

PLATE I.

Keil, Brox and Somset.

CASE 8.—CHASED BY A HOSTILE VESSEL

Plate 12

Kell Bros Lith. London.

CASE 9.— ATTACKING A VESSEL IN MOTION BY CROSSING THE BOW

## CASE 9.

ATTACKING A VESSEL IN MOTION BY CROSSING HER BOW.

In this case, the torpedo being diverged when near, will, after crossing the bow, be dragged into contact, as shown by the drawing.

Torpedoes can be used with a stern-board, if necessary. The port torpedo, in this case, will be launched on the starboard side, and the starboard on the port side.

In conclusion, it should be stated that a dark night and tempestuous weather are in favour of the attacking torpedo vessels; and these conditions are especially advantageous when attacking large, long, unwieldy vessels, and the greater the number of them together, the more easily can they be disabled or destroyed, by reason of consequent confusion. Though the sea torpedo can be used in the light of day, or darkness of night, by vessels of the present navies, armed with cannon, it is nevertheless earnestly advised that fast vessels be built of comparatively small size and cost, adapted to the service of and armed with torpedoes, by reason that such vessels can keep at sea for long periods without replenishing supplies of coals and provisions; and in conflict upon the ocean, can easily destroy or render unseaworthy vessels, how large soever they may be, and armed with any cannon and projectiles at present known. Hence the necessity of being prepared with vessels suited to the change in naval warfare, and with officers well practised in an arm which, sooner or later, will be adopted by all Maritime States, by reason of its economy and efficiency. In the tactics, here attempted to be rendered intelligible, it is presumed that the various modes of attack are by small handy vessels adapted to the service, and armed with torpedoes, against large unwieldy vessels, armed with cannon. When it shall have been clearly demonstrated, in actual war, that large vessels can be disabled or destroyed by small vessels, with something like impunity, torpedo warfare will then take another form, that of torpedo vessels against torpedo vessels, whose tactics will, in due time, be a subject for another study.

FREDERICK HARVEY,
*Commander R.N.*

Vessels adapted to the service of the sea torpedo should
be about 400 tons burthen; her extreme length, over all,
from taffrail to figure-head, about 150 feet. The form of
body to be such as to attain the greatest practicable speed.

Speed being the essential condition of a torpedo vessel, a
perfectly flush upper or weather deck, without any bulwarks, is advisable; instead of bulwarks, life-lines, sup-
ported by stanchions, supply their place to prevent acci-
dents of falling overboard. Thus fitted, there would be
nothing to hold wind that could retard speed, as there is in
vessels of ordinary build. So covered in, the vessel would
not, under any condition of weather, ship water; she
would not, from such cause, be in any danger of foundering.

The height of the weather-deck above the water-line at
midships, 9 feet; the height of the main deck above the
water-line, 18 inches; leaving a clear height between decks
of 6 feet 6 inches. There should be two water-tight bulkheads, one about 50 feet from the stem, and the other about
20 feet from the stern-post; the two water-tight bulkheads
come up to the under side of the main deck, with which the
bulkhead form perfectly water-tight compartments. In the
fore compartment, empty water-tight cases would occupy
the lower part, over which would be stowed the cork
buoys and some light resisting material, rendered unin-
flammable, so that in the event of the fore body being
ripped open below the water-line, there would be no space
for the admission of water; the trim of the vessel would
therefore be preserved. The after compartment would be
similarly stowed. There would be a capacious engine-room

E

to allow of powerful engines to work twin screws; there would also be capacious coal-bunkers and a coal-hold before the engine-room; and before the coal-hold a small hold for the stowage of cables and various articles. There would also be a pilot-house, in which would be protected the officer in command, who would be so placed as to have his orders immediately obeyed. The torpedo-room, to contain about one hundred torpedoes of various destructive powers, the weight of which may be about 10 tons, would be in the after body, and as low down as may be convenient. Upon the orlop deck, which covers the magazine, would be the towing gear, and machinery for working such gear. On the orlop deck would also be a steering wheel, by which the vessel would be steered when in action. The space between the decks of the entire length of the vessel would afford ample accommodation for officers and crew, embracing, also, stowage for provisions and means of cooking. Ventilation and light would be obtained by hatchways, fitted with skylights; and there would also be side scuttles, which, from their height above water, would admit of their being generally open. The rig would be that of a three-masted schooner, having fore, main, and mizen gaffsails, with a fore staysail and two jibs, inner and outer. When going into action, the sails would be lowered and stowed; the vessel would then be entirely under steam. To each mast there would be a yard of suitable dimensions, for the double purpose of towing the torpedoes and setting flying square sails. The rigging would not be rattled; the ascent to the masthead would be by a Jacob's ladder before the mast; there would be a small top to each masthead, principally for the use of the look-out men. The crew would be stationed upon the orlop deck, each man being provided with a life-belt. With regard to boats, there may be a small stern boat, and two larger boats, stowed on deck ; and upon going into action, gripes or lashings should be cast off so that the boats would instantly be disengaged from the vessel.

Torpedo vessels for foreign service should, under the present difficulties of keeping iron from oxidizing and fouling, be built of timber. For home service, vessels constructed of iron would be preferable, and with very reduced masts, to enable them to pass under the yards of a vessel. One or two light guns, to bring-to an unarmed vessel, and for signal purposes, on the weather-deck, and fired over all.

LONDON : PRINTED BY WILLIAM CLOWES AND SONS, STAMFORD STREET AND CHARING CROSS.

Plate 3.

Keil Bros Lith London

AN IRON CLAD FLEET SURPRISED AT SEA BY A SQUADRON OF TORPEDO CRAFT ARMED
WITH HARVEY'S SEA TORPEDOS.